New Year's Day for Cats

Written and Illustrated by Dee Smith

Copyright © 2016

Visit Deesignery.com

A brand new year is on its way.

My mind starts to wander on this day.

I wonder what new things are in store for me.

What this new year will bring, I shall soon see.

Last year was filled with moments of glee.

Next year is a surprise. A grand mystery!

What will await us in this brand new
year?

Where will time take us during its steer?

What wonderful, new and unique
friends will we make?

What magnificent journeys will we discover and take?

What amazing sights will we happily see?

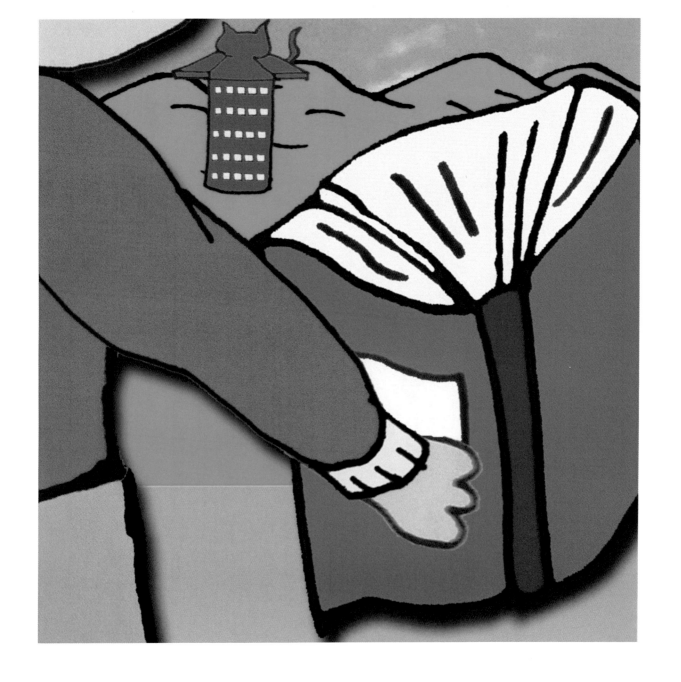

What new things will we learn,
uncover and be?

What memories will we joyfully share?

What ways will we show our family that, for them, we care?

Should I make a new year's resolution or even two?

What would I like to achieve, improve or do?

A brand new year will soon be here.

We celebrate as we wait with excitement and cheer!

Happy New Year!

The End.

Thank You!

Thank you so much for reading this book.
It means the world to me!
If you liked the book I would much appreciate if you would write a Review on Amazon. I am so thankful for each and every person supporting my dream of being a writer for children. Because you have read this book, yes that means YOU too! Thanks Again!
Stay tuned for more titles on my website Deesignery.com

Regards,
Dee

About the Author:

My name is Dee Smith. I am an Author and Illustrator. My hobbies include graphic design, puppetry, balloon twisting, drawing and of course writing. I am dedicated to my mission of keeping children entertained in fun and innovative ways.

Looking for some Winter Wonder?
Read "Winter Senses" next!

Join these cats as they explore their wintry world while using the five senses. Children will be able to relate to the winter things these cats delight in seeing, hearing, feeling, touching and tasting.

See what the Buzz is all about!
Take a journey to Bee-ville

Read this fun series about a small bee that goes on big adventures and learns along the way!

Made in United States
Orlando, FL
15 December 2023

41076963R00015